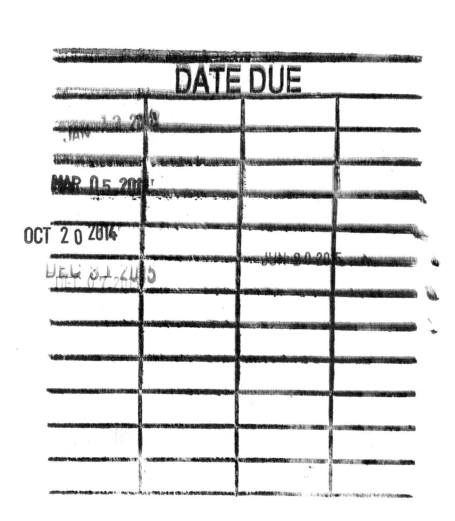

Get Around

in the Country

Get Around

in the Country

by Lee Sullivan Hill

Carolrhoda Books, Inc./Minneapolis

For Izzy, on the road again.
—L. S. H.

For more information about the photographs in this book, see the Photo Index on pages 30–32.

The photographs in this book are reproduced through the courtesy of: © Buddy Mays/Travel Stock, cover, pp. 8, 21, 22, 24, 29; © Jerry Hennen, pp. 1, 2, 11; © Bob Firth/Firth Photobank, pp. 5, 6, 14, 26, 27; © Eugene G. Schulz, pp. 7, 12, 16; © Robert Fried/Robert Fried Photography, pp. 9, 18, 20, 23; © Howard Ande, pp. 10, 17; © Sophie Dauwe/Robert Fried Photography, pp. 13, 19; © Betty Crowell, p. 25; © Elaine Little/World Photo Images, p. 28.

Carolrhoda Books, Inc., c/o The Lerner Publishing Group
241 First Avenue North, Minneapolis, MN 55401 U.S.A.

Website address: www.lernerbooks.com

Library of Congress Cataloging-in-Publication Data

Hill, Lee Sullivan, 1958–
    Get around in the country / by Lee Sullivan Hill.
      p.   cm. — (A Get around book)
    Includes index.
    Summary: Introduces some different modes of transportation used in rural areas, including cars, trucks, bicycles, sleds, ferryboats, and even walking.
    ISBN 1-57505-308-X
    1. Rural transportation—Juvenile literature. [1. Transportation.] I. Title.
II. Series: Hill, Lee Sullivan, 1958– Get around book.
    HE315.H55 1999
    388'.09173'4—dc21   98-34126

Manufactured in the United States of America
1 2 3 4 5 6 – JR – 04 03 02 01 00 99

Clip-clop through the country. Take some time to get around. Transportation gets you where you want to go.

Walking is one way to get around. Your feet can carry you to the house next door. But it might be a long hike. Places in the country are often far apart.

Some people walk a long way to do a job. They carry food from their farm to sell in town. They carry supplies back home.

Animals can help people in the country. Elephants make a heavy load look light. They pull giant logs down jungle paths. They carry people on their wide backs.

Camels take people and goods across the desert.
A camel can go days and days without drinking water.

Cars help people get around, too. Vroom! Driving a car is faster than walking or riding a camel. Cars make faraway places seem much closer.

Driving in the country can be fun. Red lights and traffic jams stay in the city. Friendly drivers wave as they pass by.

Sometimes a ride in the country gets rough. Cars and trucks can keep rolling if they have four-wheel drive. They don't get stuck in the muck.

Strong trucks can make it over bumpy roads. They haul heavy loads. They help people do their jobs.

Special kinds of trucks are built to work in the country.
Logging rigs carry logs to a sawmill.

Tanker trucks bring fresh milk to a dairy. The trucks are like big refrigerators. They keep milk cold and fresh.

Buses get around in the country, too. Passengers meet
at bus stops to share the ride. Not many people live
nearby, so buses don't come often.

School buses pick up children every morning. It takes a long time to drive from farm to farm and all the way to school in town.

Some children in the country ride bikes to school. Bike racks help students carry their books.

In some parts of the world, bikes are used more than buses or cars. Bikes cost less and never need gas. People pedal for miles and miles across the countryside.

People who live in cold places might use skis more
often than bikes. Skis glide over the top of deep snow.

Dogsleds have runners that look like skis. Teams of dogs pull the sleds. They whisk across the frozen land.

Flying is the best way to get to some faraway places.
Airplanes deliver mail and bring doctors to sick people.
Other kinds of transportation would take too long.

Some country places don't have a runway. Planes use special landing gear to float on water.

People use boats to get around on water in the country.
Swamp boats zoom across the Everglades in Florida.
A big fan pushes the boat over water and grass.

Ferryboats in Scotland carry cars and trucks across the sea. People ride inside when the weather turns rough.

There are many ways to get around in the country.
Some are just for fun. Take a horse for a ride and sit
tall in the saddle.

Or walk in the woods on your own two feet. Bring along a friend.

For fun or for work, transportation helps you get
around in the country.

Enjoy the quiet beauty along the way.

Photo Index

Cover Horse-drawn sleighs take visitors to see herds of elk at the National Elk Refuge near Jackson, Wyoming. Runners on the bottom help the sleigh ride over the snow. The horses wear horseshoes with spikes to give them traction.

Page 1 This boy is riding a dirt bike in Monument Valley, which covers parts of Arizona and Utah. The valley is a sandy plain of red sandstone and unusual rock formations. A dirt bike's wide, knobby tires grip the ground so it can travel over the rough terrain.

Page 2 Only one car at a time can make it over the Old Dewey Bridge. This narrow bridge crosses the Colorado River near Moab, Utah. Drivers usually don't have to wait *too* long to cross out here in the country.

Page 5 This buggy belongs to an Amish family near Lanesboro, Minnesota. The Amish are members of a religious group who choose to live without electricity or motorized vehicles. Families use horses for transportation and for farming.

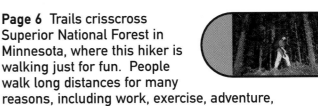

Page 6 Trails crisscross Superior National Forest in Minnesota, where this hiker is walking just for fun. People walk long distances for many reasons, including work, exercise, adventure, and to visit neighbors.

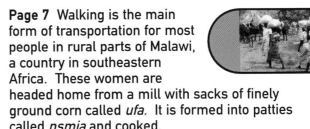

Page 7 Walking is the main form of transportation for most people in rural parts of Malawi, a country in southeastern Africa. These women are headed home from a mill with sacks of finely ground corn called *ufa*. It is formed into patties called *nsmia* and cooked.

Page 8 This Asian elephant lives in northern Thailand. Elephants can carry up to 500 pounds on their backs. People use them to pull huge logs to be sold for lumber. Read more about the elephants of Thailand in *Elephant School* by John Stewart.

Page 9 This man is riding a one-hump camel across the Sahara Desert in southern Morocco. Camels can go about eight days without water. When they finally reach water, they can gulp down 25 gallons in just a few minutes!

30

Page 10 Even when it slows down for the curves on Route 88 in Arkansas, this car travels much faster than a walker. The car will reach the town of Mena in less than half an hour. It could take *five* hours to walk the 15 miles to town.

Page 11 These friendly folks are out for a drive through the Black Hills of South Dakota in their 1959 Buick convertible. A convertible's top can be raised and locked for rainy weather. The top folds back and down for warm, sunny days.

Page 12 Roads in rural Zambia, a country in south central Africa, become muddy during the rainy season. Four-wheel-drive vehicles can get through the mess. The driving power of their engines is connected to all four of the wheels.

Page 13 Trucks travel over rough roads to reach the market in Bupuzhai, China, near the border with Vietnam. This truck carries fruits, vegetables, and baskets to sell at the market.

Page 14 This logging truck is bound for a mill, where its load of pine logs will be cut into lumber. Before trucks were invented, loggers used water for transportation. Cut logs were tossed in a river and floated downstream to the mill.

Page 15 This milk truck is leaving a dairy farm near Mankato, Minnesota, on its way to a cheese factory. The tanker has a pump that draws milk from holding tanks at the farms along its route.

Page 16 Farmers gather at a rural bus stop in Zambia, ready for a trip to the city. The buses travel through farmland between the cities of Lusaka and Chipata.

Page 17 The sun has just risen above the fields near Shabbona, Illinois. This school bus picks up its passengers early to reach school on time. Many students all over the world ride buses to school. Do you?

Page 18 These girls ride their bikes to a Muslim religious school in the rural state of Pahang, Malaysia. They ride during the warm dry season. But they stay at home during the rainy season, when roads are often flooded.

Page 19 This monk is pedaling through the mountains near Lhasa, Tibet. Bicycles are popular all over the world because they last for years and they don't need fuel, just people power.

Page 20 In Banff National Park in Alberta, Canada, snow can lie four feet deep! Cross-country skiers push-glide in a smooth, running motion. Only the toes of their ski boots hook on the skis—the heels move freely.

Page 21 This dogsled team transports goods and people in Denali National Park in Alaska. Snowmobiles have replaced most working teams. Other teams are trained for fun or to compete in dogsled races.

Page 22 This light plane sits on a grass runway in Denali National Park, Alaska. It has three-wheeled landing gear called tricycle gear. Skis are hooked on the gear when the runway is buried in snow.

Page 23 This light utility transport plane in Glendale Cove, British Columbia, is called a Twin Otter. Twin Otters are also used to fight forest fires. The floats they use for landing can take in water, then drop it on fires from above.

Page 24 This swamp boat has a flat bottom that skims across shallow waters such as those in Everglades National Park in Florida.

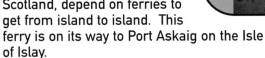

Page 25 People who live on the Inner Hebrides, small islands scattered off the west coast of Scotland, depend on ferries to get from island to island. This ferry is on its way to Port Askaig on the Isle of Islay.

Page 26 This Western-style rider is exercising a horse on a ranch in Magic Valley, Idaho. Many people ride horses because they enjoy the challenge of working with a beautiful animal that happens to weigh 1,000 pounds!

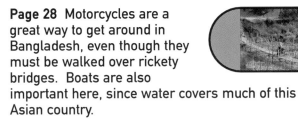

Page 27 This walker and his dog are headed down a back road near Victoria, Minnesota. Walking strengthens the heart, lungs, and leg muscles. It also exercises the mind—motion helps some people think, plan, and create.

Page 28 Motorcycles are a great way to get around in Bangladesh, even though they must be walked over rickety bridges. Boats are also important here, since water covers much of this Asian country.

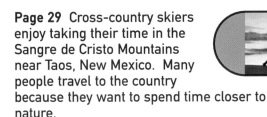

Page 29 Cross-country skiers enjoy taking their time in the Sangre de Cristo Mountains near Taos, New Mexico. Many people travel to the country because they want to spend time closer to nature.